THOMAS' SNOWY DAY

Based on *The Railway Series* by the Rev. W. Awdry

Illustrations by
Robin Davies and Creative Design

EGMONT

EGMONT

We bring stories to life

First published in Great Britain as *Terence* in 2003
Published in this edition in 2015
by Dean, an imprint of Egmont UK Limited
The Yellow Building, 1 Nicholas Road,
London W11 4AN

Thomas the Tank Engine & Friends™

CREATED BY BRITT ALLCROFT

Based on the Railway Series by the Reverend W Awdry
© 2015 Gullane (Thomas) LLC. Thomas the Tank Engine & Friends and
Thomas & Friends are trademarks of Gullane (Thomas) Limited.
Thomas the Tank Engine & Friends and Design is Reg. U.S. Pat. & Tm. Off.
© 2015 HIT Entertainment Limited.

HiT entertainment

ISBN 978 0 6035 7183 1
63581/1
Printed in Great Britain

This is a story about Terence the Tractor. When Thomas met Terence ploughing a field, he was very rude to him. But when snow came to Sodor, Thomas found out that Terence's caterpillar tracks could be Really Useful!

Autumn had arrived on the Island of Sodor. The leaves were changing from green to brown, and the fields were changing, too – from yellow stubble to brown earth. As Thomas puffed along, he heard the 'chug chug chug' of a tractor at work, close by.

"Hello!" said Thomas to the tractor. "I'm Thomas. I'm pulling a train."

"Hello!" said the tractor. "My name's Terence. I'm ploughing."

"What ugly wheels you've got!" said Thomas.

"They're not ugly – they're called caterpillars," said Terence. "I can go anywhere. I don't need rails."

"I don't want to go just anywhere," replied Thomas, huffily. "I like my rails, thank you very much."

The next time Thomas saw Terence ploughing a field, he called out to him: "You've missed a bit – over there in the corner! Silly old tractor." And he whistled rudely.

Terence carried on ploughing and didn't reply.

Winter came, and with it, dark, heavy clouds full of snow. A snow plough was fixed to Thomas, but it was heavy and uncomfortable and he hated it. He shook it and banged it until it was so dented that eventually it had to be taken off.

"You're a very naughty engine!" said his Driver, as he shut the shed door that night.

The next morning, the Driver and Fireman worked hard to mend the snow plough, but they couldn't make it fit properly. So Thomas had to set off without it.

"I don't need that stupid old thing," he said to himself. "Snow is silly soft stuff. It won't stop me."

But as he rode along, the snow kept making his wheels spin and he found it quite a struggle. He passed Terence in a field. "You seem to be having some trouble there," called out Terence. "It's a pity you don't have caterpillars – then the snow wouldn't bother you!"

This time, it was Thomas who didn't reply.

"Silly soft stuff! Silly soft stuff!" puffed Thomas as he continued on his journey – and he rushed into a tunnel. At the other end, he saw a heap of snow fallen from the sides of the cutting.

"Stupid old snow," said Thomas, and charged it.

"Cinders and ashes!" said Thomas as he ground to a halt. "I'm stuck!"

And he was.

"Oh, my wheels and coupling rods!" said Thomas, sadly. "I shall have to stay here till I'm frozen." And he began to cry.

Just then, who should come chugging along, but Terence the Tractor.

"I heard you were in trouble," said Terence. "So I've come to help."

First, Terence pulled Annie and Clarabel away from the snow drift.

"Thank you, Terence. Thank you, Terence," they said. They were very relieved to be free of the snow, and were sorry that Thomas had been so rude to Terence.

Next, Terence came back for Thomas. He pulled and pulled, but Thomas was buried so deeply in the snow that Terence wasn't strong enough to move him.

"I shall never escape," thought Thomas sadly.

The Driver and Fireman tried to dig the snow away from Thomas; but as fast as they dug, more snow slipped down.

At last Thomas' wheels were clear. But they still spun helplessly when he tried to move.

Terence tugged and slipped, and slipped and tugged. And eventually, with the most enormous effort, he dragged Thomas clear of the snow and into the tunnel.

Thomas was very grateful. "Thank you, Terence," he said. "I think your caterpillars are splendid. I'm sorry I was so rude to you before."

"My caterpillars are certainly useful," said Terence. "But I can't go very fast. I couldn't pull a passenger train like you can, Thomas."

"Well, my wheels wouldn't be much use for ploughing a field!" replied Thomas.

And with that, Terence returned to his farm, while Thomas puffed tiredly back to the engine shed.

From then on, Terence and Thomas were good friends. Whenever they passed each other, they always exchanged a cheerful greeting – and they were never rude to each other again!

GOODBYE!

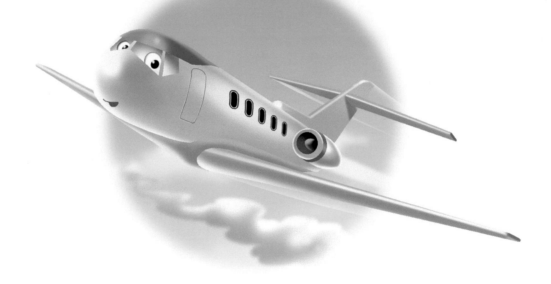